Copyright Matthew Cash/Burdizzo Books 2020

Edited by Lir

All rights reserved e reproduced in any f inclusion of brief quotations in a review, without permission in writing from the publisher. Each author retains copyright of their own individual story.

This book is a work of fiction. The characters and situations in this book are imaginary. No resemblance is intended between these characters and any persons, living or dead.

This book is sold subject to the condition that it shall not, by way of trade or otherwise, be lent, resold, hired out or otherwise circulated without the publisher's prior consent in any form or binding or cover other than that in which it is published and without similar condition including this condition being imposed on the subsequent purchaser.

Published in Great Britain in 2020 by Matthew Cash/Burdizzo Books, Walsall, UK

Keida-in the-Flames

Matthew Cash

Keida-in-the-Flames

Matthew Cash

BURDIZZO BOOKS 2020

Keida-in the-Flames

1.

The pavements were twinkling with the first signs of frost. Zoë pulled her hood over her clunky headphones and pulled the zipper up under her chin. As she scrolled through her phone, she noted that the bus was late. She hoped they hadn't just cancelled it like they often did this time of night.

A week of late shifts had come to an end and she just wanted to get home, dive into that tub of Ben & Jerry's she'd been saving all week, and get snuggled up beneath the duvet with The Witcher.

The shift at the restaurant had been catastrophic to put it lightly, a bunch of drunken idiots coming in post piss-up, loud and lecherous. Thankfully she hadn't had a groper since the summer, but there were only so many times she could smile at the same old 'harmless banter'. The week of college work and study she had planned after her night with The Witcher would come as a relief; she was intending to stay in her pyjamas as much as possible.

"Thank fuck for that!" With the bus approaching, she quickly opened the ticket app on her phone and turned up her music. *Finally, a chance to sit down.*

Zoë flashed the driver her phone, his fat bearded face and dark, sunken eyes cadaverous in the screen's glow. She raced up the stairs.

Finding a seat wasn't a problem—she was the only one on the upper deck. She collapsed into the front seat, wrapped her arms around her middle, and cursed the driver for not having the heating on. With music in her ears, and the warmth of her thick winter coat finally making a difference, she rested her eyes and let the stress of her working week float away. Zoë drifted off along with her worries.

When she opened her eyes, someone was patting her on the shoulder, a woman. Next to her was a young boy in a red baseball cap who appeared to be in some kind of distress.

His arms flailed through the air towards her, twin streamers of snot running in from a shrieking, feral face. The woman holding him back was a pretty, petite lady wearing a thick, patchwork hood. Embarrassment flushed her cheeks as she restrained the boy and said things to Zoë that she couldn't understand.

Zoë pushed back her hood and pulled down her headphones. *What the fuck's with this weird kid?* The boy seemed more frightened than aggressive, but she couldn't help asking, "Err ... what's wrong with him?"

He was a big, broad lad, almost as tall as the woman Zoë suspected was his mother, but he clutched a small stuffed Paddington Bear in one angry fist. It was obvious he had some kind of learning disability and the way she'd blurted out her question had made her sound ignorant. "Sorry, I mean ... I was asleep." She flashed a quick but awkward smile. "You made me jump!"

The woman returned the smile and barked a semi-strict 'wait' at the boy who ceased his thrashing only a little. "I'm so sorry. My son has autism and he always *has* to sit there. Would you mind?"

Zoë's hand went to her chest. "Of course," she said, scooting out of the seat, pausing to marvel at the dramatic change in the boy's face now he had seen his favourite seat was vacant.

"Gideon, say thank you to the kind lady," the woman said from beneath her knitted hood. The little boy sat down in his seat. "Thank you, Lady," he said, without looking at Zoë. He grinned and stared out of the front window, his arms stretched out in front of him, his fingers twiddling at a manic pace.

Zoë had read somewhere that that was called stimming, a way of showing physical emotion or something like that. He was cute, in a way. She sat down on the seat opposite them. "That's a great name, by the way, Gideon."

The woman smiled. "Cheers."

"Is it from the Bible?" Zoë asked. She knew there was a Gideons Bible, but that was the extent of her knowledge.

The woman pulled a face and shrugged. "Probably, but I got it from a vampire novel I was in love with as a teenager. And before you say it, it wasn't Twilight."

They both laughed at that.

"It's a cool name."

"Thank you. I usually shorten it to Gids, or Giddy, as he can be a daft sod at times."

Gideon reached forward and used a finger to quickly draw a perfect hexagon in the fogged glass before wiping it away to clear the view. Beside it, he drew an isosceles triangle and then did exactly the same thing. Zoë watched with fascination as he expertly created a variety of geometric shapes. "He's really good at drawing."

The mum shrugged again, as if what her son was doing wasn't that impressive. "He is when it comes to patterns and shapes and stuff, but ask him to draw you a picture of a cat and it'll be scribble."

" It's brilliant. Does he go to school?" Before the child's mother had a chance to answer, Zoë realised she was being an incredibly nosey bitch. "I'm sorry for asking questions, I'm just interested."

The mum's smile was genuine but Zoë could detect a hint of sadness behind it. "He goes to school, yeah. He loves it. But at the weekend, for a treat, I take him out on the late bus as he loves the dark and the lights."

"Dark and lights," echoed Gideon from beside her. He turned to Zoë, registering her for the first time since his mini meltdown. "Dark and lights!"

"He wants you to repeat what he says," his mother explained.

Zoë nodded. "Dark and lights. You like the dark and lights, Gideon?"

Gideon's smile was one of pure joy, his fingers a blur in the air. "Dark and lights, dark and lights," he sang, "buses at nights, if Gideon a good boy."

"Oh my gosh," Zoë's hands flew to her face, "He's so cute."

"Ah, he's a proper ladies' man, is my Gids.".

"Well, I'm a lady who's definitely pleased to meet him. My name's Zoë, by the way."

"I'm Faye." Mum tapped her son on the arm. "Say hello to Zoë."

Gideon turned to Zoë, once more showing his angelic grin. "Hello to Zoë."

Zoë laughed hard, happy that this awesome mum and her even more awesome kid had woken her up on her last trip home of the week. As the windows clouded over with their commingled breath and the bus pulled into the next stop, she wondered what shapes Gideon would draw next.

A few seconds passed whilst the bus driver picked up some more passengers and Zoë studied Faye's unusual hoodie, admiring its unique bohemian design. Patchworked sections of various shapes and colours were stitched together: stars, flowers, rainbows, intricate stick figurines. Pictures within pictures. She had seen similar clothing at hippy markets and on adverts on Facebook but this garment looked like a one-off. It really was beautifully made. She leaned in as they watched Gideon happily trace diamonds on the glass. "I have to say — I love your top."

Faye plucked at the material as if she hadn't even noticed she was wearing it. "Oh, thanks, I've had this shabby old thing for years, used to be my mum's. It's like wearing a duvet."

"I love the patterns, and all the details," Zoë said, and noticed even more images on the front when she turned to her.

Faye nodded. "It is special, she used to call it her witch's cloak, ha-ha! She reckoned she was a Wiccan."

"Oh, wow," Zoë said, genuinely intrigued, just as a group of teenage boys thundered up the stairs and across the upper deck hard enough to cause the bus to shake.

One of them laughed unnecessarily loud at something, sounding like a demented pirate, and Gideon flinched in his seat at the sudden interruption to their tranquil journey. Rolling her eyes, Faye muttered something under her breath and rested a hand on her son's shoulder.

The bus started moving again and the repetitive strains of *heavy bass and lyrics overloaded with expletives* travelled to the front, the boys having to shout to hear each other.

"Jesus Christ," Faye seethed. "Inconsiderate pigs."

Zoë refused to be intimidated and chose to ignore their racket. "So, are you into that stuff, too?"

"What stuff?" Faye said, her annoyance still obvious as her eyes darted to the group of lads at the back.

"Wiccan, pagan stuff?" Zoë asked.

Faye shook her head. "The type of stuff my mother was into was all about runes, symbols and whatnot, made no sense to me—but Gids used to like looking at the patterns in her books. They're full of weird things called sigils and … Right, that's it!" Faye jumped up and stormed towards the back of the bus. Zoë felt herself go cold at the prospect of confrontation.

"Don't you fucking dare smoke weed near my son, do you hear? He's got autism!" Faye raged, as the first wafts of marijuana reached Zoë.

She saw the boys for the first time: a typical street gang, hooded and of indeterminable age, somewhere in their teens, probably. The apparent ringleader sat centre-aisle; legs spread. His pale face looked mean: jaw jutting, eyes wide, nostrils flared. He took a drag on a thick roll-up and blew the smoke towards Faye before nipping the burning tip between his fingers.

"Thank you," Faye said, and nervously sat back down. Zoë had time to briefly see the relief on her new friend's face before someone from the back of the bus called out, "We don't want your mong to get even more monged."

A raucous cacophony of hoots, wails, whistles and laughter filled the bus.

Faye sprang to her feet, eyes wide with rage, and Zoë instinctively thrust out her arm to block the gangway and prevent her from running to the back of the bus.

"You fucking chav cunt!" Faye shrieked over Zoë's shoulder; it took all her strength to stop her getting past. Behind Faye, Gideon looked on, his eyes deep blue pools of fear, hands glued against his ears. "No Mummy shouting!" He screamed. "No Mummy shouting! No Mummy shouting! No Mummy shouting!"

The commotion sent the boys into further bouts of laughter, coupled with poor imitations of Gideon's mantra.

Zoë was sure of one thing, at least. That this wasn't just tonight. That this wasn't a new experience for Gideon and his Mum. That this was the sort of shit they'd had to endure day-after-day, year-after-year.

"Please, Faye," Zoë pleaded. "Just ignore them. You don't know what they're capable of."

Faye sneered at the boys and bared her teeth at them but slowly sat back down.

Tears soon came.

Gideon, starting to calm now that his mum's shouting had stopped, went back to his window gazing.

"I just wish I could take him out in the daytime, you know?" Faye said, between sobs.

"Why can't you? Surely it would be safer?"

"I do try — but he's a stickler for routine, and like I say, he seems to prefer the dark. There's less people about."

"Yeah, but the people that are about aren't exactly sociable."

"There's just as many during the day where kids like Gids are concerned," sighed Faye, "but they just blend in with the ordinary ones. The nice ones, the genuine ones, are rarer than unicorn tears."

Zoë reached across and put her arm around Faye's shoulder. "You're doing a great j—"

Someone screamed, "DYKES!" and a can of something exploded against the front windscreen directly above Gideon's head, showering the little boy in froth and making him jolt backwards in shock. "No, Mummy, no wet! Not bath day, not bath day!"

"You fucking cunts!" Faye batted Zoë's arm away before she had a chance to stop her. She stormed down to the back of the bus and her right foot shot between the ringleader's legs.

Keida-in the-Flames

2.

Gideon thrashed about, half on the seat, half on the floor, his red face screaming garbled words as he beat the walls with his fists. Zoë got up as Faye was suddenly brought down to the deck by several boys.

The ringleader got to his feet. He was a gangly fucker — his hood brushed the ceiling. He swung out a foot until it connected with Faye's face and a spray of red sprinkled the floor. Red with clumps of white. Grabbing his crotch, he towered over her, his cohorts bringing up the rear. "Ahmed, Ste, Neil, make sure that fit bitch don't get off the bus — she's the main course."

Three of the boys came Zoë's way and she turned towards the stairs. *Surely the driver will be able to do something?*

All the time Gideon was squealing and she knew she couldn't leave him up there with them. *Why can't the driver hear what's going on? Don't they have mirrors and cameras on these bloody things?*

"Stay away from me," Zoë threatened. That was when one of them opened his coat to show a long handle jutting out of his waistband. He withdrew it to show her it was attached to a thick blade.

Zoë let out a laugh. "You're like fucking twelve and you're carrying a fucking machete."

The boy spat in her face. Another one of the lads, who didn't appear to be much older — but old enough to grow a pathetic fuzz over his upper lip, grinned lecherously at her. "Yo, don't go fucking with Ahmed, bitch, or he'll fuck with you."

"Fucking fuck you up your white ass, bitch!" Said the boy with the machete, spitting again.

Zoë tried to hold back the tears, but there were too many and the dam broke. "Please, this little boy, he has autism, his name is Gideon. Don't hurt him or his mum, I think they're all each other's got."

The third lad, heavily-acned, sniggered and crowed over his shoulder, "Eh, Reaper, the spacker kid's called Gideon, what kind of a fucking name is that?"

Zoë was horrified when she turned to see who he was talking to. The ringleader had Faye's comatose body bent over the back of one of the seats and was busy doing something behind her.

Zoë's cries for help only exacerbated things. Screaming, Gideon threw himself around with even more ferocity, grazing his forehead against the metal underneath the seating, and the three boys rushed her.

Ahmed, who she assumed was the only one with a weapon, stayed behind, brandishing it like the warrior he thought he was, whilst the other two boys threw her against the front window. One drove his fist into her belly and she was sure she was going to die. She crumpled to the floor opposite the terrified little boy and wished she had never got on that fucking bus.

Keida-in the-Flames

3.

"Come on, bitch — wake up." They hauled Zoë onto the seat and she started to come to.

She risked a look back and saw the boy called Reaper cutting at Faye's clothing with a knife.

"Shut up! Stop screamin'!" Ahmed stood in the gangway kicking at Gideon's gyrating feet, which only antagonised him all the more.

Zoë turned to the other boys. "Please don't hurt him!"

The boy with the bumfluff on his face pointed at Gideon. "Then get him to shut the fuck up."

Zoë got out of the seat and Ahmed blocked her way, holding the machete blade up between them. "Excuse me, please."

He reached forward and grabbed her left breast, hard. Zoë closed her eyes just in time to hear him spit and feel his hot, thick phlegm slide down her cheek. She wiped at it with her sleeve.

"It'll be my spunk later, bitch," he said, letting go and moving out of her way to stand with his friends. "Now, you got five minutes to shut the freak up before I chop him up."

The kid —that's all he really was— turned to his mates and chuckled as they bumped fists and high-fived each other. Zoë went to try and help the severely troubled kid she had only just met, whilst his mother was getting raped—again— at the back of the bus.

4.

Instinct told her the worst hadn't happened yet. Reaper had a clump of Faye's grey-blonde hair in one hand as he slapped at her bloodied face with the other, shouting in her ear for her to wake up. Zoë fought through the tears and the fear and forced a semblance of a smile as she crouched near to Gideon.

"Gideon," she called carefully, staying clear of his flailing limbs, "it's me, Zoë. Everything's going to be alright, okay?"

Struggling with invisible demons, the boy paid her no attention. The graze on his forehead had sent a curtain of blood over his eyebrows and cheeks, which were already starting to swell. He was frantic and putting everything he had into his fight. His trousers were soaked with what she presumed was urine, or the drink that had burst.

This was way out of her comfort zone.

The knuckles on both his hands were bleeding from beating at the walls, so she grabbed at one of his arms to try and stop him. It was the wrong thing to do.

He growled at her in frustration and his head shot forward, teeth snapping at her like something out of a zombie flick. She recoiled, expecting him to attack her — but once he saw she wasn't in his personal space he let her be. But the gang had other ideas.

Ahmed kicked his foot out, striking Gideon in the ribs. The boy rolled onto his side, suddenly blank and silent.

"No, you fucking animal!" Zoë screamed, and threw herself over the boy before Ahmed could kick him again. "You leave him alone!"

"Don't you tell us what to do, bitch," sneered the boy with the acne, "it shut the little fucker up, didn't it?"

Ahmed laughed as Gideon started to shake in Zoë's arms.

A wet, unearthly scream came from the back of the bus, but cut off as quickly as it started.

Faye was awake.

From her position in the aisle at the front, Zoë could see Faye's naked arms thrashing about in the air as her fingers tried to grab, rake and claw at anyone — anything— that got in her way.

"GIDEON!" Faye screamed through a mouthful of blood. Faye somehow slipped free of the two boys, but they had stripped her naked. She got about three feet down the bus before Reaper, the lanky ringleader, grabbed her by the hair and started to yank her back down the aisle.

"Mummy, Mummy, no!" Gideon suddenly whined from beneath Zoë's armpit, reaching out for his mother.

"Don't ... let ... him ... see —" were the last words Zoë heard from Faye before she was dragged to the back seat and lost in a melee of slapping, grunting meat sounds.

Don't let him see.

Gideon struggled to free himself from Zoë. This was not an autistic fit; this time he wanted to get to his mother. She had to distract him; she couldn't let him witness the horrors at the back of the bus. On the floor below the seats, discarded in the terror, lay his stuffed Paddington Bear. Zoë snatched it up and held it to her chest. "Look, Gideon," she said, unable to stop the tears and the fear in her voice. "Look who I've found."

A small flicker of happiness lit up the boy's blue eyes. "Paddington!"

The three other boys had turned to watch the fun at the back of the bus. Zoë saw the windows had fogged almost white with their combined breath, and had an idea. "Shall we get Paddington to draw some shapes on the window?"

Gideon's was amazed, as if what she had suggested was the best idea in the world. His little hands clapped excitedly and he shouted, "Paddington do shapes, Paddington do shapes! Dark and lights, dark and lights. Paddington. Paddington!"

Helping Gideon to his feet, she spotted one of Faye's legs splayed in an awkward position over the back of one of the chairs and quickly blocked it from his view. They faced the huge window spanning the front of the bus and she pressed one of Paddington's paws against the glass and drew a rough triangle in the condensation. She turned to Gideon. "Your turn."

Gideon bounced up and down on his toes, oblivious to anything else, his fixation paramount. He took the little teddy bear in the blue duffle coat. "Gideon do one of Nanny's book patterns?"

Zoë nodded and all her energy left her. She fell onto the seat as the boy traced intricate shapes and sigils on the glass. Without thinking, she lazily lifted her arm and pressed her thumb against a red button on one of the hanging posts. Above Gideon, the word 'stopping' glowed red.

Laughter came from the back, and her three sentries returned.

"The driver's Reaper's cousin, bitch. We do this shit every fucking week, who do you think tips us off?" Neil said, pointing at the front window. "Kid's really good at that shit, he'd be sick at tagging, I reckon."

Zoë was amazed at the progression Gideon had made on his pattern in such a short space of time — three-quarters of the window were taken up with moons, stars, wavy lines, zigzags, curves, what appeared to be suns — and even eyes and mouths. She wondered what the hell kind of patterns he had seen in his grandmother's books.

She turned to the boy who was watching Gideon work with genuine fascination, "Please, don't hurt him. I think I know what you mean to do to me and his mum, but please, I beg you, don't hurt him."

He looked back at her and she was sure she detected the onset of tears. "I don't call the shots, man. Reaper does."

"What's your name?" Zoë asked. Ahmed the machete-wielding psycho and his acne-pocked sidekick had turned back to the scenes of barbarism, Faye's screaming increasing as the others took their turns with her.

The boy took his eyes off Gideon's masterpiece, his cheeks flushed. "I ain't saying, you think I'm stupid?"

"Big man up there has already said Ahmed, Neil and Ste. Ahmed has made himself known, so which one are you?"

He let out a hollow laugh. "Neil. So what? Even if he lets you go, nobody is gonna get us, we're untouchable, Reaper says."

If Reaper lets you go … She tried not to let the fear show. "You can't honestly rape and kill two women on a fucking bus!"

The forced laughter came again, but so did a few tears, and the boy swatted at them with his fingers. "Reaper has done this before."

So, these are the stakes, then? Zoë perched on the edge of the seat. She was going to be brutally gang-raped and killed by a bunch of teenage boys for their own sordid kicks. She plunged her hands deep into her coat pockets and regretted every time her paranoid father had insisted she carried some kind of makeshift weapon. He was full of self-defence information he had learned from his mates down the pub or online, almost always unreliable sources.

His speciality was making weapons out of everyday objects that you would normally carry around with you, that way you couldn't get into too much trouble with the police if you really hurt someone.

"Zo, a can of Deep Heat basically has the same ingredients as pepper spray. Always keep a can in your gym bag."

As if she would go to the bloody gym, for fuck's sake.

"Keys! Stick 'em between your fingers and punch the bastard in the face. It'll tear his fucking cheek off!"

She didn't even carry her own set half the time, they normally sat gathering dust on her bedside table. She wasn't much more than an irresponsible teen herself.

"Even a pen can be used as a weapon …"

Zoë reached for her work bag.

"What you doing?" Neil said, peering over her shoulder. He turned away when Faye's shrieks were cut off with a wet, gargling sound followed by intense, insane laughter.

"Getting a tissue for Gideon's face," she replied, congratulating herself on her quick thinking. She felt around in her bag for the packet of Kleenex she always carried, found the biro in the pocket of her work shirt, uncapped it and slid it up her coat sleeve. She made a point of showing the tissues to her guard and moved towards the little boy. "You don't have to do anything to him." Zoë wiped away the blood from Gideon's face. "You can all see he's locked in his own world, look at him."

Gideon was oblivious to having his face wiped, the flashes of passing streetlights twinkling in his wide, fascinated eyes as he concentrated on his drawings. The pattern was all he cared about at that moment. It was all he saw. And all he felt was the cool glass beneath his fingertip.

Neil slumped in the chair and pressed his palms against his eyes. "My little brother was autistic, he died when I was ten."

Zoë stepped away from Gideon, clutching the bloody tissue. At the back of the bus, Faye staggered to her feet, her back to the gangway, supported by Reaper and one of his friends. Bruised and scratched, she stood on unsteady feet before Ahmed and Ste manhandled her onto another seat.

There was nothing Zoë could do for Faye at the moment but she would do everything she could to try and save her child. The boy with the facial fuzz was weeping into his hands. *Now is the time.* Zoë wrapped her fingers around the pen in her pocket, mentally practicing plunging the pointed end into the fleshy dough on the side of the bastard's neck.

Now is the time.

Zoë took her hand out of her coat pocket and raised it in the air.

Three things happened at once:

Gideon added a semi-circular curve at the lower right-hand corner of the window.

Faye broke away from her rapists and threw herself over the backs of the nearest seats, hands reaching for her son, yelling, "No, Gideon, stop!"

And the bus stopped abruptly, sending everyone crashing forwards into headrests and windows.

5.

When the bus came to a complete standstill in an instant, Zoë was thrown forwards into the front windscreen. Her head and arm collided with the plexiglass, her shoulder crunched, cracking timber, something splintered near her collarbone and shifted beneath the skin. Her forehead slammed against Gideon's sigils, freckling them with blood. She rebounded onto the dirty floor, screaming out as she landed on her damaged arm and it made even more ungodly sounds. Despite the agony, she forced herself to roll onto her back.

"Fuckin' 'ell, lads." The gang members were busy picking themselves up. Ahmed's machete lay unattended mere feet away from Zoë and he grinned maliciously at her misfortune as he bent to retrieve it. He was limping on his left side; she was glad to see that one of them had been injured.

There was something so callous and animalistic in the boy's eyes, she wondered what kind of upbringing it took to instil that in someone so young. If he was in pain, he wasn't going to show it—he would just hide it behind bravado and that ever-present sneer.

That sneering face turned completely blank when he looked beyond Zoë and turned to get the attention of the other boys. Faye slumped out from between a pair of seats. Dishevelled and deranged, she crawled on bloodied hands and knees up the gangway ahead of the boys, dribbling blood. As she looked up at Zoë, her face took on the same blank expression.

Zoë braced herself for some horrific scene of even bloodier carnage; it was obvious the bus had crashed even though she had felt nothing collide with them.

Neil, the ginger kid with the facial fuzz, sat across from her, and for a second, everything appeared normal. Then she noticed the pinkish clumps on his coat and saw that there was nothing from the neck up aside from a mush of spurting gore. The remnants of his head were embedded in the front window, which, incredibly, was still intact.

No wonder they stared.

Oh my god, what about Gideon? Vomit rose in Zoë's throat as she turned around to look for the little autistic boy.

"We're all going to die." Faye spoke slowly and clearly as Zoë's face took on the same blank expression as the others.

Keida-in the-Flames

6.

Gideon floated in the air as though some invisible force had hoisted him up beneath the armpits. He appeared unconscious but otherwise unscathed: eyes closed, chubby chin tucked into his chest, red baseball cap slightly askew. His feet dangled just above the sill of the bus window, and he clutched Paddington Bear tightly by the paw. A soft, unearthly glow came from the front of the bus; a sickly spectrum ranging from a white that spoke of dark winter days to headache-inducing lilacs, violets and purples before fading into the pitch of night.

The boys stood behind Faye, all wearing similar expressions of sagging shock. Tears streamed from the mother's puffed eyes as she saw what was happening in front of them.

Faye whimpered something through bloody gums and pushed past Zoë as if she wasn't even there.

Zoë trailed behind the naked, beaten lady. Everything felt surreal, drugged. Around her, the air itself heady with exotic zests and spices. Through heavy eyelids, she saw fine tendrils of purple vapour wisp and curl in through an open window. She wondered if they had crashed into something toxic, a lorry transporting chemicals of some kind — were they being poisoned? When she moved her arm, the uninjured one, it was sluggish and leaden, as though she were moving through water.

Faye came to her son's dangling feet and reached up to wrap her arms around his waist. She buried her face in his stomach to blanket her scream.

The purple haze rolled in through the opened windows and Zoë covered her mouth and nose with the cuff of her coat sleeve.

A couple of the boys shifted behind her.

Ahmed broke the silence. "The fuck's he doing?"

"Shut the fuck up!" Reaper snapped. Zoë could hear the fear and uncertainty in his voice before the bluster returned and took over.

"WHAT THE FUCK IS GOING ON?" He shouted.

In front of the bus, the white light began to strobe, swathing the interior of the bus. Faye turned to the others, looking like a lilac-skinned witch with a deranged grin. She seemed entirely toothless; it was as if the forty-something woman had turned into a wrinkled hag, gummy and rotten.

Faye's laughter was an asthmatic hiss. "You boys are all dead!" She said, pointing a finger—black with her own blood— at the five figures behind Zoë. A brief glimmer of genuine sorrow passed over her when she addressed Zoë. "I'm so sorry you got mixed up in this, all you've done is help, but no one else can care for my son."

"What's happening, Faye?" Zoë said softly, suddenly frightened of the poor wretched woman.

Violet light reflected in Faye's eyes as she turned her face towards the front of the bus and the vast intricate pattern that covered the window. Zoë could see something through the sigils on the glass—something was on fire out there, something that burned with a dancing white flame.

"Gideon has called Her," Faye said quietly, staring into the flickering fire. "He has called The Keida-in-the-Flames." She looked through Gideon's finger marks on the glass. "She will be here soon."

"Get him the fuck down," Reaper barked at Ahmed and the acne-covered youth. "I'm going downstairs to see what the fuck we crashed into. We need to go before the coppers get here." He touched a hand on the decapitated ginger boy's shoulder, his fingers amongst the gruel. "Rest in peace, Neil."

He turned to his goons. "Don't let them go anywhere 'til I've checked down below." The gang were trying hard to ignore Faye's insane babbling and get past the levitating eight-year-old. Reaper's cold blue eyes studied him with cool indifference. He swung around into the stairwell and spat out one last comment before he went below. "Get that fucking kid down."

Faye squatted in a fighter's stance, her hooked, bloodied fingers ready to scratch and gouge. She had fought her attackers hard; she would fight even harder to stop them hurting her son.

Zoë's numbness beginning to thaw, the boys moved towards them. The sickening light painted their faces: purple-and-lilac masks with blackened eyes. Ahmed raised the machete level with his face.

There are benefits of this happening on a bus. Zoë's father spoke in her mind — his survival instincts had rubbed off in some way. *Narrow aisles. Only one of the bastards can come at you at a time.*

Zoë slipped the pen back into her palm and mapped the exact point on Ahmed's neck where she would drive it in. *First, take out the one with the weapon.*

Ahmed went straight for Gideon, and Faye flew at him — fingers raking the air, a beaten woman making her last stand. Faye dug her fingernails into his cheek and they stripped back thick curls of flesh. The machete chopped down once and severed two of Faye's fingers. Zoë struck Ahmed with the biro. She brought it down into the side of his neck where it protruded momentarily like a tranquilizer dart before it was lost in the fight.

Ahmed roared and pounced back, holding the machete out before him. The wound on his cheek bled more freely than the one Zoë had made with the pen. Faye knelt on the floor in agony, sobbing uncontrollably as she searched for the energy to pick herself up to continue the attack.

Ahmed stood over Faye and raised the machete.

Ste whimpered quietly at his shoulder. "Ahmed, man, you shouldn't, not until Reaper says."

He nudged the boy away and scowled back down at Faye.

"No!" Zoë screamed, fastening a hand around Faye's ankle. The skin was slick with blood but she pulled on it as hard as she could, managing to haul Faye back a couple of inches and startle her out of her frenzy. Gideon twitched a foot against her back and the light behind her became so bright she was forced to close her eyes.

Keida-in the-Flames

7.

The bus became enveloped by sound and light. A distorted harmony, an out-of-sync choir singing in tongues with a backing orchestra of wind instruments blown by hurricanes, the fluttering of one billion wings. An intense hallucination flashed behind Zoë's eyes: a head-on collision between the bus and a flock of angels, with blood, feathers, gold, and the light of God. Gideon danced upon her shoulders. She held onto his legs and realised he was suspended in the air, held up by invisible arms. She clung to him as the sound and the light and the sudden, overpowering aroma of burning flowers flooded the bus.

The light began to soften and the boys retreated to the back of the bus.

"She is here!" Faye said, enraptured. Zoë detected movement through her eyelids. Only a small part of her believed it might be the emergency services; her intuition told her something else was coming. Something else entirely.

From a distance it resembled a burning torch, its heart white, the flames a spectrum of lilac and violet. It shone through the purple fog like the flaming torch of a lynch mob leader—but as it came towards the bus, Zoë could see a dancing silhouette inside it, becoming clearer as it drifted through the mist.

A wingless angel. It danced as though the very air below it was its catwalk and podium. Flames licked at opal skin; its hair was pure white light and flowed like weeds in water. The strange dancer slowed once it reached the bus window. All around the figure, like a barely perceptible aura, faint lilac flames swaddled— but never burned.

Zoë studied its face, beautifully defined with enviable elfin perfection; miniscule rivulets of violet fire glittered along albino white eyelashes. The vision had no distinguishing features other than its intense beauty and humanoid shape, with nothing to define its gender—but Zoë instantly considered it *she*.

When she opened her eyes, they glowed luminescent purple and had no irises—Zoë felt an unusual sense of peace beneath her gaze. She pressed her hand against the glass and recoiled. The surface had changed texture even though it still looked the same. The glass was pliant, membranous, and cold. Zoë pulled her hand away from the window and the glass stayed stuck to her palm, sucking on her skin. She stepped back and wiped a hand on her coat even though the window left no residue. Gideon's hand-drawn mural remained unmarked. The thing outside the window pressed her palm to the other side of the glass and her fingers flowed through as if she were testing the temperature of a lake. Becoming one with the surface, she slowly drifted all the way in.

Zoë moved back in awe and nearly tripped over Faye, who was on her knees, hands clasped together as if in prayer. "She is so beautiful," whispered Faye, tears clearing the blood from her face.

The women watched in amazement as the figure dipped a long, slender leg onto the bus deck as if she were stepping into a pool. An overgrown fairy-tale imp, she perched herself on the windowsill and seemed to take in Faye. A white hand reached out and delicately caressed one of Gideon's dangling exposed ankles. She smiled, revealing dark teeth of purple glass and a tongue that flickered blue. The murky well of the stairs beckoned her; the gang leader had been down there a few minutes. He had probably abandoned them all, his friends included.

Zoë's survival instincts kicked in and she felt herself descending to the lower deck before she even noticed the smell.

There hadn't been many passengers downstairs, but they were now charred so black they had become one with the molten plastics and metals of the furnishings. Reaper barely seemed to notice, continuing instead to pry the lock of the emergency door. The knuckles of the hand bearing his gang tattoo were swollen and bloody.

Zoë turned to run from the burned passengers but stopped in her tracks as she caught something moving. The bus driver. Still alive.

He had been a big, rough guy, a typical bus driver. She vaguely remembered him as a balding, bearded man, but now he was entirely smooth, all hairs singed from his skin. His clothes little more than black embers, his skin was red and weeping. Parts of his skin had welded to the plexiglass of the cabin partition, thick clots of bubbling orange fat oozing through the gaps where his gigantic gut had pressed against the door and popped like a sausage in a pan. His mouth — by now a gloopy orifice of molten skin — began to move, but nary a sound came out. Even though his eyes had boiled in their sockets, he had somehow detected her movement. Zoë scanned the walls, what was left of the cabin, everywhere, until she found the button for the door release.

"It doesn't work. There's no way out." Reaper sat amongst the shadows at the back of the bus. "What the fuck do you think I've been trying to do? I don't know what the fuck kinda shit you two and that kid are into but if you don't call it off, you're all going to die." He pressed a button on his knife and retracted the blade.

"We're all going to die." Zoë corrected him and collapsed onto the nearest seat.

Reaper shook his head in obnoxious denial, "Nah, not me. I'm getting out of here. Me and my boys always get out in one piece."

"One of your boys currently has his brains sliding down the window upstairs," Zoë laughed. "And have you seen the fucking bus driver?"

Reaper shrugged, "Horses for courses, man. Flesh is flesh, theirs was obviously weak. The strongest will survive."

"You're not strong. You hunt in a pack and prey on the weak and defenceless."

"You'll see just how strong we really are, bitch, once I've figured out how to get off this fucking bus," Reaper sneered and got to his feet, flicking open his blade.

If she had angered him, she didn't care anymore, her shoulder hurt and she wanted an end to the madness—one way or another.

"Get up," he said, yanking her to her feet and pushing her towards the stairs. "Let's end this."

Keida-in the-Flames

8.

Nobody moved. Everyone aboard the top deck waited as if in suspended animation, just like the autistic kid.

With wide eyes, Reaper studied the thing on the windowsill, making sure he was shielded behind Zoë. Faye remained knelt in worship, her son still suspended in mid-air.

The ethereal being gazed over them with an angel's serenity, her palms crossed upon one knee. When she spoke her voice was elemental, like the wind trying to form vowels and consonants through long, desiccated vocal cords. "I am The Keida-in-the-Flames. All but the Caller and the Guardian shall come."

Her words brought the other boys from the rear of the bus. They huddled at their leader's shoulders.

"What the fuck are you on about, love?" Reaper said, with mock laughter.

The Keida's eyes sparkled as she repeated herself from her throne.

Shaking, Zoë extended a hand— something told her this creature deserved some respect. "Excuse me, but just to make sure you are aware, this little boy is the one who called you."

"Shut the fuck up, bitch!" Snapped Reaper.

The Keida laughed, but her placid expression turned serious when she looked at Reaper. "I know my caller."

Zoë felt purple eyes on her.

"I value the truth. Most try to lie, beg and bargain. Your honesty has been noted." The Keida slid off the sill and onto her toes, the lilac flames encasing her like fine silks. She reached out a flawless hand in Faye's direction. "Mother, please stand."

"You're that thing's mum?"

"Hush, rapist!" The Keida sprayed, her spittle sparks from an old-fashioned tinderbox. "She is a mother. I am not born."

Reaper strode forward, chest puffed out and eyes wide. "Who the fuck do you think you are, talking to me like that?" He thumped at his breast. "I'm not scared of you. I know how this kind of shit works. You're nothing without fear — and me and my boys ain't scared of nothing, do you hear me, you fucking fairy-tale freak? Nothing."

Behind him, the four boys gathered close, bolstered by his bravado. Ahmed brandished the machete, the manic glint back in his eye.

The Keida laughed again and slid off the sill. Her left foot landed with the grace of a ballet dancer — but the right slipped in the liquid from the drink the boys had thrown at Gideon.

Zoë cringed as she saw her foot turn in on itself and heard a loud snap as navy blue bone shards splintered through her delicate skin. A hideous, painful noise escaped her—a combination of sonar and whale song— and beat at their eardrums. She fell to one knee. Beside her, Gideon slowly dropped to the floor.

Without even knowing what this entity was, Zoë had instinctively chosen her as the lesser of the two evils aboard. She squeezed past Faye and rushed to the fallen one's aid. "Let me help you," she said, reaching out but not daring to touch her. Although she could feel no heat, and nothing about this creature followed the rules of logic, she was taking no risks.

The Keida lifted her pointed chin and smiled. "Observe, Zoë Jones."

The fact that this thing knew her name, and her sudden apparent recovery, had no time to register as one of the boys grabbed Zoë by the hair and dragged her backwards into the nearest seat.

"Get these cunts out of my way," Reaper ordered, storming over to the fallen fairy and spitting in her upturned face, taking note that the saliva sizzled before it even made contact with her skin.

"Ahmed," he called, without taking his eyes off the entity. "Come here."

The machete-wielding psychopath came to his side.

Keida-in the-Flames

9.

Zoë fought the boy who had dragged her to the seat. He was one of Reaper's right-hand men, and had been up the back of the bus when they'd taken turns with Faye.

He pushed her back with his huge hands, sweat running from his face and dripping onto her. He was heavy-set, and stank. Faye began to shriek, a never-ending scream. Zoë caught a reflection in a window — the machete blade rising near the ceiling, Reaper's determined mask painted in the Keida's spectral glow before he sliced downward. A wet thunk followed by a masculine grunt and throaty laughter. Then came Reaper's triumphant voice. "Flesh is flesh! Flesh is flesh!" The gang joined in with their boss's chant as the sounds of stomping feet and the chop-chop-chop of the blade turned Faye's cries into defeated whimpers as she witnessed the destruction of the beautiful creature her son had beckoned.

The guy on top of Zoë clamped her wrists with one hand using the other to fumble with the buttons of her jeans. Over the boy's broad shoulder, Reaper walked past, the heroic monster slayer speckled with the blood of his kill.

"Kill the old bitch and the kid. Have fun with the young one first," he muttered, between exerted breaths. Zoë struggled with the boy on top of her. "Damo's already got first dibs, by the looks of things." He caught her eye— and with a wink and a smile that exposed his crooked teeth, thick with plaque, reminded her, "Flesh is flesh, babe."

"BUT I AM NOT FLESH!" The shrieking anger of the Keida-in-the-Flames came at such a volume it made Zoë's eardrums whine.

A wave of heat, the opening of a door to the inferno, tore through the interior of the bus.

The air rippled with the intense temperature and a blast of invisible energy ripped the boy from on top of her and sent him rolling over the headrests. Zoë clung to the upholstery and felt the hell-breath scorch away the thick thermal layers of her coat and smelled the singeing of her own hair. Any courage she'd had left was burned to the ground with the Keida's fire; she buried her face into the seat and waited to die.

It took a long time to happen but when she felt a hand on her shoulder, Zoë caved in and wept.

"It's okay." It was Faye. She had retrieved some of her ruined clothes; the hooded cardigan Zoë had admired was wrapped tightly around her waist.

"Has that *thing* gone?"

Faye shook her head. "But there might be enough to satisfy her without us." She cocked a thumb toward the rear of the bus. Zoë perched between the seats and saw the five boys sat, backs straight, eyes forward, all paying attention to their teacher.

They were immobile, fixated. The Keida was before them, immaculate, uninjured.

Zoë sought out Gideon. The little autistic boy who had summoned this ethereal being sat in his favourite seat, facing away from them. Zoë turned back to the Keida—even if she had the energy, there was no way off this bus without her permission. She stayed beside Faye whilst the woman from another realm went about her lesson.

"First, before your mortal punishment, I shall show your three jurors your crimes." The Keida glared at each of the boys in turn, lingering on Reaper and Ahmed before flicking her violet eyes at Zoë. "Pay close attention before you pass judgment."

What the hell is the point of this? Zoë already knew they were as guilty as fuck.

10.

The Keida dropped to her knees. Pigments flooded her ghostly skin; fleshy hues at first but then the deep purples and reds of bruises, abrasions, and finger marks. Her hair hung limp, a yellow mess. The boys' faces paled as they beheld her transformation as the Keida, now a naked teenage girl, reached out towards them with broken hands. She crawled towards them, sometimes on all fours, sometimes dragging herself across the floor on bent-back fingernails. Her appearance flashed through a kaleidoscope of different women of all ages, ethnicities and sizes, a physical manifestation of their collective rape, until she reached the bloody feet of the gang leader, where she begged and pleaded for her life in a dozen different voices. Reaper sneered at her and laughed a lunatic's hiss. He struck out with the toe of his shoe, kicking the side of her jaw, and she rolled away — still flickering between incarnations of victims before crumpling beneath the seats.

The form of an emaciated old lady in sagging, wet clothes pointed a rheumatoid finger up at Reaper. Her toothless mouth opened, and black blood poured and sprayed the floor as she hacked and wheezed. One sliver of blue amidst a face that resembled bruised, misshapen fruit passed a single tear as the Keida forced words out of the old woman's loose, shattered jaw. "Your own grandmother."

"Fuck you. You don't know what it was like, the shit I used to have to put up with. My own dad used to—" The gang leader clamped his mouth shut before he would divulge anything else, and turned away from the vision. The boys wouldn't meet his eyes.

"You mugged and raped your own grandmother," The Keida sang, back in her original form. "Preying on the weak makes you feel empowered. Torturing, abusing, manipulating...You've never had a fair fight in your life."

"No, no, no!" Reaper started, weakness bringing an unusual childishness to his voice. "There was that time—"

"There was that time, there was that time," the Keida taunted. She strode towards him, her facial features hardening into a broad, masculine jawline, her hair receding to a grey shadow. A tall, haggard man soon stood in her place and continued her belittling mantra. He thrust a hand toward Reaper's chest but the boy recoiled and fell backwards into his friends. "Always knew you were a fucking pussy. Never stood up to me, did you?" The man grinned maliciously at him — the family resemblance was strong. Reaper cowered at the back of the bus as the Keida's latest manifestation casually moved towards him.

Reaper's father addressed the gang. "My son. My own flesh and blood. A fucking pox on society."

"He stole from his own family, killed his own dog." He pointed a nicotine-yellow fingertip at the space below the chair where moments before they had witnessed Reaper's half-dead grandmother.

"You saw what he did to my mother. If I had known, I would have finished him off myself. I said whoever did this to my mum would get their throat slit." He glared at his son. "Didn't I?"

"Stop him," Reaper said, cowering behind his four guardians.

"They're not going to help you, Son, don't you get that? They've seen what you did to your own family. They know just how low you will go."

A wide blade blocked his path and Ahmed stepped between his leader and the spectre of his father. The boy's dark eyes were impenetrable. "You are just a ghost, nothing real. You can't hurt us, not properly. You can tease us, torment us, but that's all you can do, innit? Otherwise you would have done it by now. Your kind live off fear, or use someone else to act on your behalf. It's true, isn't it?"

The spectre's expression faltered and its features began to melt. Ahmed moved forward, emboldened by its gradual retreat. He stopped the machete millimetres from the Keida's chest, and flashed a sinister smile. "I'm not scared of you."

"Go on, Ahmed!" Reaper encouraged as they all watched the boy drive the monster away.

"We're not scared of you," Ahmed said with added vehemence, thrusting the machete tip with each syllable. The Keida continued to back away, her transitional appearance settling back into its original form. As she came level with Zoë and Faye, they could see her tremble —as though a creature such as this could experience fear.

"And," Ahmed added, looking over at Gideon, "I know how to make you go back to where you came from."

"Don't you dare," Faye shrieked, lunging at the boy. He knocked her away with a fist and moved closer to Gideon.

Zoë grabbed at Ahmed's arm but he flung her back into her seat. The Keida stood to the side staring blankly, while Gideon's eyes started moving rapidly beneath their lids.

"I know how to end this." Ahmed said, lifting the machete above the autistic boy's head. Faye leapt onto his back, her fingers scratching at his face and reopening the claw marks that had only just began to clot. Zoë reached again for the machete, the Keida's blood still glistening on the metal.

"Fuck off, cunts." Ahmed chomped his teeth at Faye's searching fingers and the bloodied stumps that oozed red, the jagged split bones ripping at his lips.

A quick glance to the back of the bus told Zoë that this fight was futile; Reaper had gotten over the shock of seeing his father and was coming to Ahmed's aid. Faye was weakening by the second and Zoë couldn't hold the boy's arm much longer. The blade came closer to Gideon.

A pair of small hands slapped onto the back of Gideon's headrest, making Zoë scream and let go of the thrashing Asian boy. All fight left Ahmed as he froze at the vision behind her shoulder.

"I thought you only liked little girls." The Keida had taken the form of an Indian toddler, her hair pinned back with a pair of red clips, and wearing a Little Mermaid swimming costume. She peeped between the seats at Ahmed with huge eyes that seemed too big for her head: dark and portentous, but full of childish innocence. "Not fair, Ahmed. You never played fair."

Ahmed locked eyes with the girl.

"I always did as you told me but you never did what you promised." The girl's lower lip began to tremble.

"Shut up," Ahmed whispered.

"It's why I was going to tell Daddy what you used to do to Mya and me."

"Shut up!" Ahmed screamed. "You're not real. You just live off fear, just like all the shittest fucking monsters."

Zoë clambered up off the floor, she had to stop him before he thought about hurting Gideon again. Her bad shoulder had rendered that arm useless so she couldn't get up quick enough. Faye was on the other side of the deck in a similar — if not worse — state, and Reaper and the other three had arrived. But then a miracle happened.

11.

Damo threw himself at Ahmed, and in one swift motion, managed to take the machete from the younger boy's grasp. Ste, who'd dared to tackle Reaper, had already fallen to the floor and was methodically being beaten by his leader for the sheer mutinous audacity of it all.

The little Indian girl giggled at the blood-splattered mayhem as if it were nothing.

"Enough!" Damo shouted, seizing authority.

Reaper glared, his face red with rage. "You're fucking dead."

"No," Damo said. "You forced us into this shit, Bro. We were too scared to say no." Tears welled up in his eyes. "It was always you pair from the start, and now she, whatever that thing is, has proven it." When he looked at the Indian girl, genuine sadness took over. "What did Ahmed do to you?"

The girl seemed surprised to be addressed, and all the usual bashfulness of a normal toddler crept into her face and voice. She looked at the floor. "He would touch me and make me touch him but one day he did something else, something different that hurt me bad. I bleeded lots. I said I would tell our mummy and daddy what he did to me and my sister Mya but he pushed me under the water in the paddling pool until I went to sleep."

"You fucking—" Ste muttered, and turned away from the vision as she began to cry.

"It's not true," Ahmed pleaded. "It's all lies, man. That thing is the devil, the master of lies."

"Yeah, come on," Reaper said, changing tack. "You think me and Ahmed would do something like that to kids and old people, for fuck's sake? Really?"

"Flesh is flesh," Said Ste, trembling. "It was yours and Ahmed's motto. That, *and any hole is a goal,*" he added.

"Never thought you'd take that so literally." Damo said.

"Cunts," Spat Reaper. "So, what the fuck are you going to do now? You think you have the answer, is that it?"

Damo nodded. "The only ones that need to leave here are the two women and the boy."

Their leader's face paled, and for once he remained speechless.

"What we've all done is unforgivable." Damo stated, looking at Zoë. Ste nodded in agreement.

Damo turned to the Indian girl. "Please," he said, "whatever you are, I know you have the power to send those three back safely. You can have us without a fight. Please just send the boy and the women back."

She was silent whilst she contemplated his offer, her small forehead crumpling before a wide grin cracked her face and her eyes rolled back into her head and shone with the Keida's violet vibrancy. She stretched herself out on the seat, her back arching as she blended back into her original form. Amused, she took them all in approvingly like they had all passed some kind of test. "Oh, such noble, courageous men," she said, her words dripping with sarcasm, "but just like many of your kind, you did not listen to my words before."

All must come with me except the Caller and the Guardian, Zoë remembered.

"You can't do anything. You just want to watch us kill each other." Reaper said, walking away from Ste. "All you can do is visual mind games." He tapped a finger to his temple. "Sure, you can move stuff a little, manipulate what we see, but that's all. For all I know, this is all a fucking hallucination. We could all be lying dead in a ditch somewhere." He marched towards the Keida; his arms splayed wide. "If you can do something, just fucking do it —because I've had enough."

The Keida stepped forward.

"Kill me!" Reaper shrieked at the top of his lungs, his face contorting with the ferocity of the volume.

The Keida raised a hand slowly upwards towards Reaper's face, never taking her eyes off his for a second. The gang leader tried to remain defiant but started to tremble.

"J-just do it," he stammered.

"Bang!" The Keida said, miming a gun. "I've always hated the male of your species. So impatient." Leaving Reaper gasping for breath, she moved closer to Damo and Ste, who were still holding onto Ahmed. "Very well. So begins our second lesson."

12.

"My boys," she said with a sultry smile, "such glorious specimens of men. Thugs, Neanderthals, preying on the weak and defenceless. Rapists. Murderers. You have the audacity to act like gods!" She approached Damo and stroked his face until blisters started to bubble. His eyes watered but he didn't move— none of them did, they seemed to be suspended in space. Reaper stood confrontational, the kid with the knife was poised with his weapon frozen in front of him, and Damo and Ste held their hostage against the machete's blade.

"Flesh is flesh," the Keida hissed their collective motto back at them. "And you've all had your fair share, haven't you? Now I'm going to demonstrate how I can manipulate yours." The Keida nodded to Zoë and Faye. "All but the Caller must come with me— but our only innocent here needs a Guardian, someone who will stay by his side for the rest of his life." Her smile was sympathetic, as if she could feel such emotion. "That is something you two must decide upon very soon."

The Keida's implications earlier had left Zoë speechless, and the time to make that decision was almost up. Faye grasped her hand tightly. "Will you look after my son for me?"

"What? I can't. He's autistic." Zoë hated herself for saying that, and regretted the hurt on Faye's face. Hated the fact that she would rather face an uncertain death than the alternative. "You can't be serious? You can't go through all this and leave him!"

Faye nodded sadly. "I don't want to live with your death on my conscience and the memories of the things they did to me. Please. You're young, you deserve to live. It's all my fault. If my mother didn't have all those stupid books— I never for the life of me believed in any of it."

Zoë gripped Faye's hand. "There has to be another way. Can't these things be bartered with? It seems like she's only here for the really bad people, like some kind of avenging angel."

"Hush!" The Keida snapped in their direction and Zoë felt a force clamp her mouth shut. Wide-eyed, she realised she had no power over her own body. Once, she'd suffered sleep paralysis, and this felt the same — aside from the fact she was standing and able to move her eyes.

"Flesh is flesh," the Keida whispered, and all five boys cried out in unison as their FIF gang tattoos glowed purple and branded into their flesh.

"Flesh is flesh," the Keida repeated as the gang members broke away from one another erratically. "Such a limited, human thing to say."

The boys jerked towards nearby seats, slaves to their puppet master.

"Flesh is flesh," the Keida smiled. "Allow me to demonstrate the fragility of the sacks of meat and bone you so desperately lust after. How easily they come apart."

Zoë could only watch with morbid curiosity.

Suddenly, as though the Keida had freed them to fight, the boys were released from their trances and it was their instinct to stand up. Reaper moved towards the Keida, and wasting no time at all, he picked up Ahmed's fallen machete. But his movements quickly became sluggish.

Ahmed took to his feet and immediately fell to his knees. His hands failed to support him and he face-planted the floor. Damo stumbled like a drunkard and fell over him. Ste and Knife-Boy stayed rooted to their seats, not daring—or able— to move.

"You've entered the first stages of human decomposition—your cells are destroying themselves at an alarming rate."

"Fuck you," Reaper slurred, trying to drag himself towards her. The discolouration started to blossom around his mouth, and his lips began to crack and weep. High-speed deterioration, part living horror, part nature documentary. The gang leader's stomach puffed up over the waistband of his tracksuit trousers, pregnant with the accumulation of his internal gases.

Zoë could smell them. This would be what zombies would smell like.

Ahmed flopped onto his side, a thick froth spilling from his mouth and nose.

Damo, the boy who had tried to save them, sat on his haunches, screaming at his extended belly. He clawed at it with black hands, simultaneously crying and laughing, a spreading wet patch soaking through the front of his trousers. Zoë turned away when his frantic scrabbling at the pressure-filled balloon of his gut caused it to expose and the newly released gases escaped from a wide abdominal gash.

Their skin marbled with advanced rot, the last of their flesh liquifying beneath their sagging skin and seeping out of every orifice.

Reaper's zombified corpse slid across through the rotten slurry, desperately reaching for the Keida's foot before finally coming to a standstill.

The sweet but rancid smell of rot and burst innards filled the bus. Zoë covered her mouth and nose with a coat sleeve. At the Keida's feet, the five dried-up gang members still miraculously twitched with life. She couldn't believe they had survived that. *How could they?* The Keida had made them, that's how. She saw the muscles bunch in the Keida's slender back as she raised her arms in worship. "Rise."

The gang members got to their feet like puppets from a bad stop-motion animation. The thin sheen of flames that wrapped the Keida started to fade as the undead boys rose. Was using all this energy sapping her of her power?

The boys rippled as they rotted in reverse; all the pain appeared to be equally as traumatic. Their bodies rejuvenated and returned to how they once were, young and healthy —but for the most part, frightened.

"Why?" Reaper screamed, falling to his knees in tears, finally beaten. "Why don't you just kill us?"

"Oh, Brave Leader," The Keida said, running her fingers over his closely cropped hair, burning his scalp. He flinched and attempted to move but she clasped on to his head, smoke rising. She ignored his struggle and thrashing arms, and held him in place. "You haven't learned anything, have you? You live by the rule 'Flesh is Flesh'." She squeezed his head a little harder, making him squeal. "And I want to feel your flesh part beneath my fingers."

As she tore her hand from Reaper's head, he fell away, a blistering red handprint covering his scalp. She crouched down and picked up Ahmed's machete. "Unfortunately, that is not what I'm here for. I am not here to kill you." The Keida turned to where Faye sat cradling Gideon, who was stirring from whatever unnatural sleep he had been put into.

"Dark and lights, dark and lights..." He sang quietly.

The Keida offered the blade to Faye and Zoë. "Have you chosen?"

Faye looked at Zoë out of her destroyed face, her eyes almost swollen shut. Her jaw was most definitely fractured, but not half as much as her mind.

Zoë was numb. The trauma of the night had started to lower its blanket and slow her senses.

"Who is the caller's guardian?" The Keida asked, her voice soft and mesmerising.

"Look after my son, please," Faye said, resting a hand on Zoë's knee. "You'll get to know him, understand his needs, if you just pay close attention."

No, Zoë thought, recoiling. She couldn't care for the little boy. It was absurd. Even if she somehow managed to get past the legal technicalities, she would have to sacrifice everything to look after someone else's child. It wasn't fair. It wasn't her fault. She didn't ask for any of this. But what was the alternative? To die, and go to whatever realm the Keida-in-the-Flames came from? "I can't," she stammered.

"Please," Faye begged. "I can't live with what has happened — and what is about to happen." Faye stood up, shed her tattered hippy cardigan and took the proffered machete.

"Faye! Please! I can't look after him!" Zoë screamed. If only the kid was normal. "I'm sorry, I'm sorry."

The Keida blocked her path and held out a burning palm. Faye passed them. The machete was massive in her hands. She approached the dumbstruck boys.

"The choice has been made, Zoë Jones," said the Keida, her eyes glowing bright. "Sit next to your son."

"He's not my—" was all Zoë managed to shout before her body was manipulated by invisible means and she was forced down into the seat beside Gideon.

From behind her came an intense violet glow and the sounds of the boys screaming. Soon, these sounds were joined with wet chopping, hideous shrieks and after what seemed an eternity, exhausted panting and the drop of something heavy and metallic.

"Pretty," Gideon said, rubbing a fingertip down the window at the purple fog that curled in wisps beyond the bus. Zoë turned away from him, free to move, and stumbled away. The Keida waited on the stairwell for her; nothing had changed. Zoë threw herself at the creature's mercy and was surprised at how cold the entity felt, like she was burned out. "Please, take me instead."

"No. The choice has been made. Everything is as it should be." The Keida stroked her hair, and it didn't catch fire. Zoë allowed herself to be led back up the stairs to where Faye was sitting next to Gideon.

The back of the bus was an abattoir — and Faye had been its butcher.

Zoë watched Faye whisper heartfelt sentiments to a child who most likely didn't understand them, his fingers flicking back and forth in a blur of excitement. Paddington Bear tucked beneath one arm, Gideon looked towards her and smiled sweetly and she tried her best to swallow the hatred she held for him. It was all his fault. At the back of her mind she still prayed that this was all a vivid hallucination, despite the pain.

The Keida pointed to the front seat, and Zoë sat. The Keida walked hand-in-hand with Faye towards the window where Gideon's finger-painted sigils and symbols began to run. Gideon resumed revelling in his weekly treat on the night bus, and smiled and looked out of the window. "Dark and lights, dark and lights, buses at night."

When Faye turned back to Zoë, she could see any injuries, blemishes, wrinkles and other signs of age begin to vanish from her face and body as if she were slowly being scrubbed away.

The Keida and Faye stepped up onto the bus windowsill and passed through it like ghosts.

"Pretty ladies gone now," Gideon said, waving and smearing a streak through the patterns in the condensation.

Zoë made out streetlights and traffic before she saw the reflection looking back at her. It was Faye's, not hers. She groaned and looked down at herself, at the tattered hippy cardigan and the body that was now twenty years older than it should be. Knowledge, everything about Faye and her special son Gideon, came in an instant, flooding her mind. Everything about the protections his grandmother had put in place, the pacts and rituals and sacrifices to keep her precious grandson safe. Where she now lived with Gideon, how old he really was —and what would happen if she ever stopped loving him.

Author Biography

Matthew Cash, or Matty-Bob Cash, as he is known to most, was born and raised in Suffolk, which is the setting for his debut novel, Pinprick. He is compiler and editor of Death by Chocolate, a chocoholic horror anthology, and the 12Days Anthology, head of Burdizzo Books and Burdizzo Bards, and has numerous releases on Kindle and several collections in paperback.

He has always written stories since he first learned to write, and most, although not all, tend to slip into the many-layered murky depths of the Horror genre.

His influences —from childhood to present day—include: Roald Dahl, James Herbert, Clive Barker, Stephen King, and Stephen Laws, to name but a few.

More recently, he enjoys the work of Adam Nevill, F.R Tallis, Michael Bray, Gary Fry, William Meikle and Iain Rob Wright (who featured Matty-Bob in his famous A-Z of Horror title, M is For Matty-Bob, plus Matthew wrote his own version of events, which was included as a bonus).

He is a father of two, a husband of one, and a zookeeper of numerous fur babies.

You can find him here:

www.facebook.com/pinprickbymatthewcash

https://www.amazon.co.uk/-/e/B010MQTWKK

PINPRICK

All villages have their secrets, and Brantham is no different.

Twenty-years ago, after foolish risk-taking turned into tragedy, Shane left the rural community under a cloud of suspicion and rumour. Events from that night remain unexplained, memories erased, questions unanswered. Now a notorious politician, he returns to his birthplace when the offer from a property developer is too good to refuse. With big plans to haul Brantham into the 21st century, the developers have already made a devastating impact on the once quaint village. But then the headaches begin, followed by the nightmarish visions.

Soon, Shane wishes he had never returned, as Brantham reveals its ugly secret.

VIRGIN AND THE HUNTER

Hi, I'm God. And I have a confession to make.

I live with my two best friends and the girl of my dreams, Persephone.

When opportunity knocks, we are usually down the pub having a few drinks, or we'll hang out in Christchurch Park until it gets dark, then go home to do college stuff. Even though I struggle a bit financially, life is good, carefree.

Well, it was.

Things have started going downhill recently, from the moment I started killing people.

KRACKERJACK

Five people wake up in a warehouse, bound to chairs.

Before each of them, tacked to the wall, are their witness testimonies.

They each played a part in labelling one of Britain's most loved family entertainers a paedophile and sex offender.

Clearly, revenge is the reason they have been brought here, but the man they accused is supposed to be dead.

Opportunity knocks, and Diddy Dave Diamond has one last game show to host — and it's a knockout.

KRACKERJACK2

Ever wondered what would happen if a celebrity faked their own death and decided they had changed their minds?

Two years ago, publicly shunned comedian Diddy Dave Diamond convinced the nation that he was dead, only to return from beyond the grave to seek retribution on those who ruined his career and tainted his legacy.

Innocent or not, only one person survived Diddy Dave Diamond's last ever game show, but the forfeit prize was imprisonment for similar alleged crimes.

Prison is not kind to inmates with those type of convictions, as the sole survivor finds out, but there's a sudden glimmer of hope.

Someone has surfaced in the public eye claiming to be the dead comedian.

FUR

The old-aged pensioners of Boxford are very set in their ways, loyal to each other and their daily routines. With families and loved ones either moved on to pastures new or maybe even the next life, these folk can become dependent on one another.

But what happens when the natural ailments of old age begin to take their toll?

What if they were given the opportunity to heal, and overcome the things that make everyday life less tolerable?

What if they were given this ability without their consent?

When a group of local thugs attack the village's wealthy Victor Krauss, they unwittingly create a maelstrom of events that not only could destroy their home but everyone in and around it.

Are the old folk the cause or the cure of the horrors?

Other Releases by Matthew Cash

Novels

Virgin and the Hunter

Pinprick

Novellas

Ankle Biters

KrackerJack

KrackerJack 2

Clinton Reed's Fat

Illness

Hell and Sebastian

Waiting for Godfrey

Deadbeard

The Cat Came Back

Frosty [coming 2019]

Short Stories

Why Can't I Be You?

Slugs and Snails and Puppydog Tails

OldTimers

Hunt the C*nt

Non-fiction
From Whale-Boy to Aqua-man

Anthologies Compiled and Edited by Matthew Cash of Burdizzo Books
Death by Chocolate
12 Days STOCKING FILLERS
12 Days: 2016
12 Days: 2017
The Reverend Burdizzo's Hymnbook*
SPARKS*
Under the Weather [with Em Dehaney & Back Road Books]
Burdizzo Mix Tape Vol.1*
*with Em Dehaney

Anthologies Featuring Matthew Cash
Rejected for Content 3: Vicious Vengeance
JEApers Creepers
Full Moon Slaughter
Full Moon Slaughter 2
Down the Rabbit Hole: Tales of Insanity

Visions From the Void [edited by Jonathan Butcher & Em Dehaney]

Collections
The Cash Compendium Volume One
The Cash Compendium Continuity
Come and Raise Demons [poetry]

Website:
www.Facebook.com/pinprickbymatthewcash
Copyright © Matthew Cash 2020

Printed in Great Britain
by Amazon